ALL OF ME

A POEM FOR EVERY EMOTION

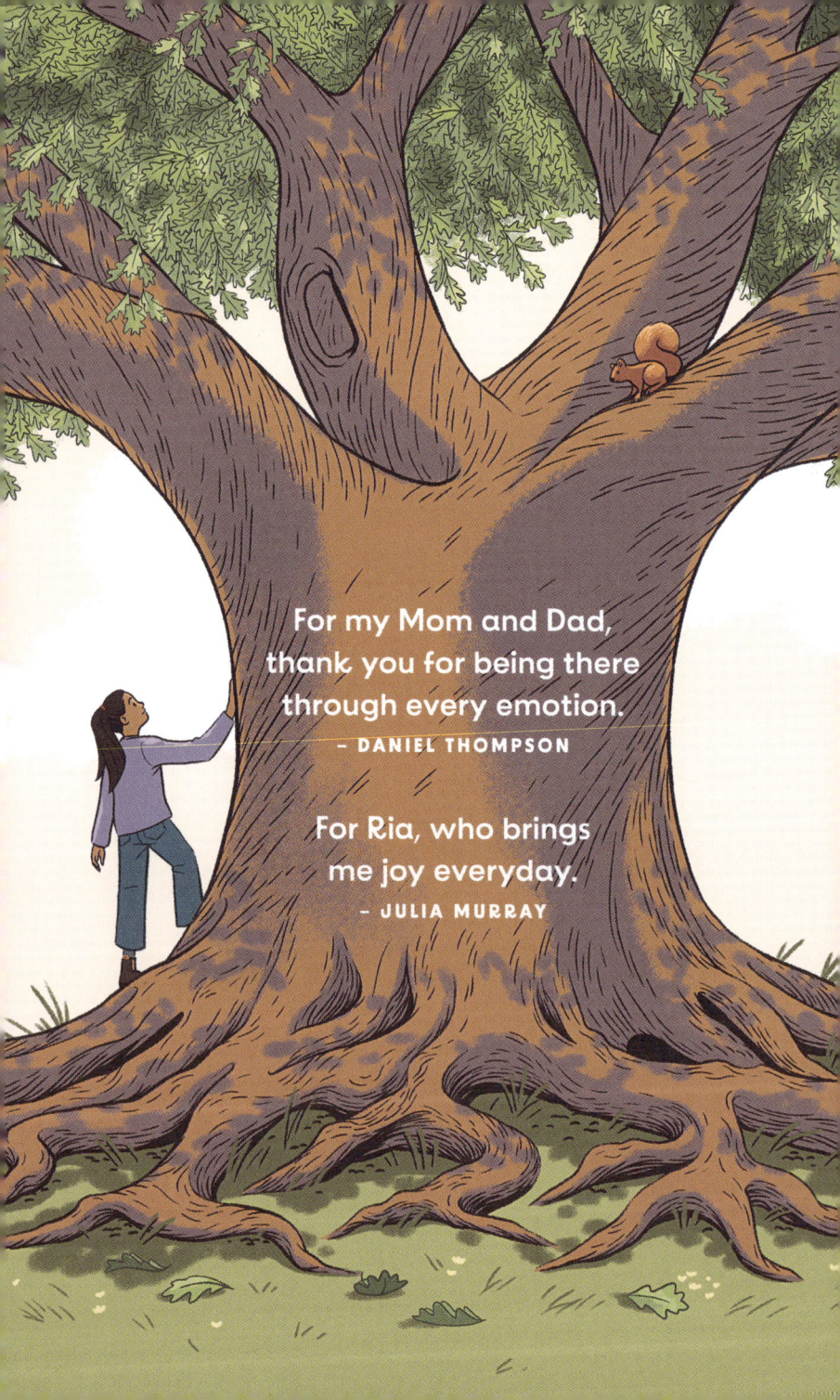

For my Mom and Dad,
thank you for being there
through every emotion.
— DANIEL THOMPSON

For Ria, who brings
me joy everyday.
— JULIA MURRAY

ALL OF ME

A POEM FOR EVERY EMOTION

written by
Daniel Thompson

illustrated by
Julia Murray

Contents

ALL OF ME

All of me is certain
That there's more than one of me!
And I can't say from day to day
Which me I'm going to be.

There are more than two,
Much more than three,
Even more than forty-four.
And every time I count the MEs
I end up finding more.

There's happy me who smiles a lot,
That's a me you'd like to meet,
An angry me who shouts and snarls,
And stomps with fiery feet.

There's a me who's always laughing,
There's a me who's very shy,
There's another me who's curious,
Forever asking why.

There's a me who's glum and full of tears,
Head slumped and feeling low,
An anxious me so timid,
They forget to say hello.

There's a lazy me who's sleepy,
Who drives mum round the bend,
A grinning me you'll only see
Whilst playing with my friends.

There's a me who always thinks too much,
Another not enough,
A me who's scared to be alone,
And one who thinks they're tough.

There's a grumpy-in-the-mornings me,
An angry-without-warnings me,
A brimming-with-excitement me,
A searching-for-enlightenment me.

Yes, all of me is certain
That there's more than one of me!
And I can't say from day to day
Which me you're going to see.

Today you might meet one of me,
Tomorrow two or three,
Or eight or nine, and you might find
They don't always agree.

But what I've come to realise,
As odd as it may be,
It really does take all of them
To make up ALL OF ME!

THE POWER OF HELLO

Feeling shy

The word 'hello' may come and go
As quickly as a wink,
But those five letters, said aloud,
Are stronger than you'd think.

Hello might be a new best friend,
Hello might understand,
Hello might be the first day of
Adventures yet unplanned.

Hello might be that hobby
You've been waiting to discover,
Hello might be a mystery
That you'll help to uncover.

Hello might be the answer
To that question you've been asking,
Hello might be your calling
To a joy that's everlasting.

Of course, there are a lot of times
Hello just means hello,
But if you never utter it,
Well then you'll never know.

And yes, it's hard to find that word
When you are feeling shy,
But stop! Before you walk away,
Here's a few more you could try...

Hola, bonjour, hallo, or hej,
Konnichiwa, shalom, g'day,
Ni hao, salaam, or namaste,
Or howdy partner, how's your day?

Pick your fave, be brave, then go!
The rest of your life
Might start with hello.

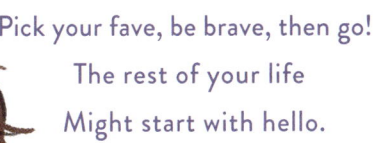

FiT FOR KiNGS

Feeling grateful

Here's a list of all the things
That once were only fit for kings:

- Hot water in your bath or shower
- Food to eat at any hour
- Inside toilets that aren't just pots
- At least three pairs of pants and socks
- A carriage to carry you on your way
- Clean water to drink, every day

And here's a list of all the things
That once were only dreamt by kings:

- Planes to fly like birds above
- Phones to call the ones you love
- All we know on tiny computers
- Radios, TVs, Wi-Fi routers
- A cure when you're ill that's a pill you can swallow
- Libraries full up with books you can borrow

Now look at your life, is it fit for a king?
Do you have half the things that are listed?
If you do, then know you
Are the envy of most
Of the humans who've ever existed.

HOME iS...

Feeling content

Home is where your house is,
It's the place in which you live.
But home is made of so much more
Than addresses that we give.

Home might be a feeling,
Or a kind and friendly face.
It could be your favourite people,
Or a calm and peaceful place.

Home is where you're happy,
It's a place where you feel strong.
Home's where you can be yourself
And feel like you belong.

Home's your favourite dinner,
Served with smiles on the side.
Home is looking at your friends
And filling up with pride.

Home is laughing endlessly,
Until your cheeks are sore.
Home's reading your favourite book
In your favourite nook once more.

Home is where you're comfortable
To share what's in your head.
Home's your favourite teddy bear
When you're curled up in your bed.

Home is where you're welcome,
Where you're made to feel unique.
Home's the local football team
You play for every week.

Home's the words, "I love you"
From the lips of those who care.
Home's a cat sat on your lap,
In a worn and comfy chair.

Home is where you feel safe,
It's your go-to happy place.
Home is warmth inside your heart
And a smile on your face.

It's a fizzing in the belly,
Like the static on the telly.
It's a whizz-bang spinning
Catherine wheel.
It's wibbling, wobbling jelly.

It's that moment of unease
You feel right before you sneeze.
It's a volcanic eruption,
It's a dread that makes you freeze.

It's untamed anticipation
In your vast imagination.
It's a string of twinkling
Christmas lights
In full illumination.

But it fizzes for a reason,
And that reason is that you
Care deeply for the outcome
Of what you're about to do.

So if you're feeling nervous,
Don't be scared of the effects.
Just take a breath, do your best,
Then see what happens next!

The first rule of Self-Love Club is always be yourself.
I'm afraid we cannot let you in if you are someone else.

The second rule of Self-Love Club is celebrate each win.
Whatever you achieve today, enjoy it with a grin.

The third rule of Self-Love Club is give yourself a break.
Not every day is perfect, so allow yourself mistakes.

The fourth rule of Self-Love Club is remember to be kind.
Love your body, love your mind, love the 'you' you find.

The fifth rule of Self-Love Club is accept a compliment.
If someone's kind to you, then smile, and take it how it's meant.

The sixth rule of Self-Love Club is share talent, don't be shy.
If you love it, we do too! Be brave, give things a try.

The final rule of Self-Love Club is believe in who you are.
Set your goals and trust your soul, and you will go so far.

FACE YOUR FEAR

Feeling scared

Fear exists in many types:
A shadowy room on stormy nights,
Crashing noises, flashing lights,
Enclosed spaces, spiders, heights.

Yes, if you let it, fear can grow
Outwards, upwards, down below,
Until you stand up and say NO!
Reclaim your brain and let it go!

Face your fears, and you will find
Each fear you face is left behind,
And as they fade you will in time,
Realise most fear is in your mind.

WORDS MATTER

It's widely suspected
By those in the know,
That treating plants kindly
Might help them to grow.

And not just with water
Or a spot in the sun,
But by speaking kind words
While the watering's done.

Yes, as odd as it seems,
If you talk to your plants
In a way that is kind
It may help them advance.

Now, if that is true,
And if all things are equal,
Imagine how kind words
Affect other people.

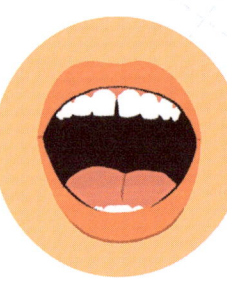

THE SUM

puddle + wellies
fish + chips
TV + sofa
hula hoop + hips

kite + wind
treasure + map
blanket + fort
cat + lap

music + ears
birthday + cake
paper + crayons
milk + shake

book + nook
magic + trick
snow + sledge
dog + stick

OF SMiLES

Feeling happy

woods + walk

sun + pool

chocolate + mouth

foot + ball

stars + night

castle + sand

popcorn + movie

controller + hand

friends + lunchtime

ice + cream

singing + dancing

sports + team

bubble + wand

daisy + chain

family + dinner

board + game

Whenever you start something new,
At first you won't know what to do,
But trust yourself and see it through...
One day you'll be an oak.

Plant your seed in soil below,
Then give it time and let it grow,
Until the first shoots start to show...
One day you'll be an oak.

At first, you'll likely feel exposed,
To the howling wind each time it blows,
But hold your ground and stay composed...
One day you'll be an oak.

And as you settle in, you'll learn
Your roots have spread to hold you firm,
And you will stand without concern...
One day you'll be an oak.

A towering trunk, now strong and still,
No longer scared of winter's chill.
It took great faith and iron will...
But now you are an oak.

BECAUSE YOU CAN

Feeling kind

Whatever you do on this planet of blue,

If you end up the star or the fan,

Be good because you should be,

And be kind because you can.

Wherever you are, be it near or far,
From Peru to the edge of Sudan,
Be good because you should be,
And be kind because you can.

No matter the season, regardless of reason,
Whatever your journey or plan,
Be good because you should be,
And be kind because you can.

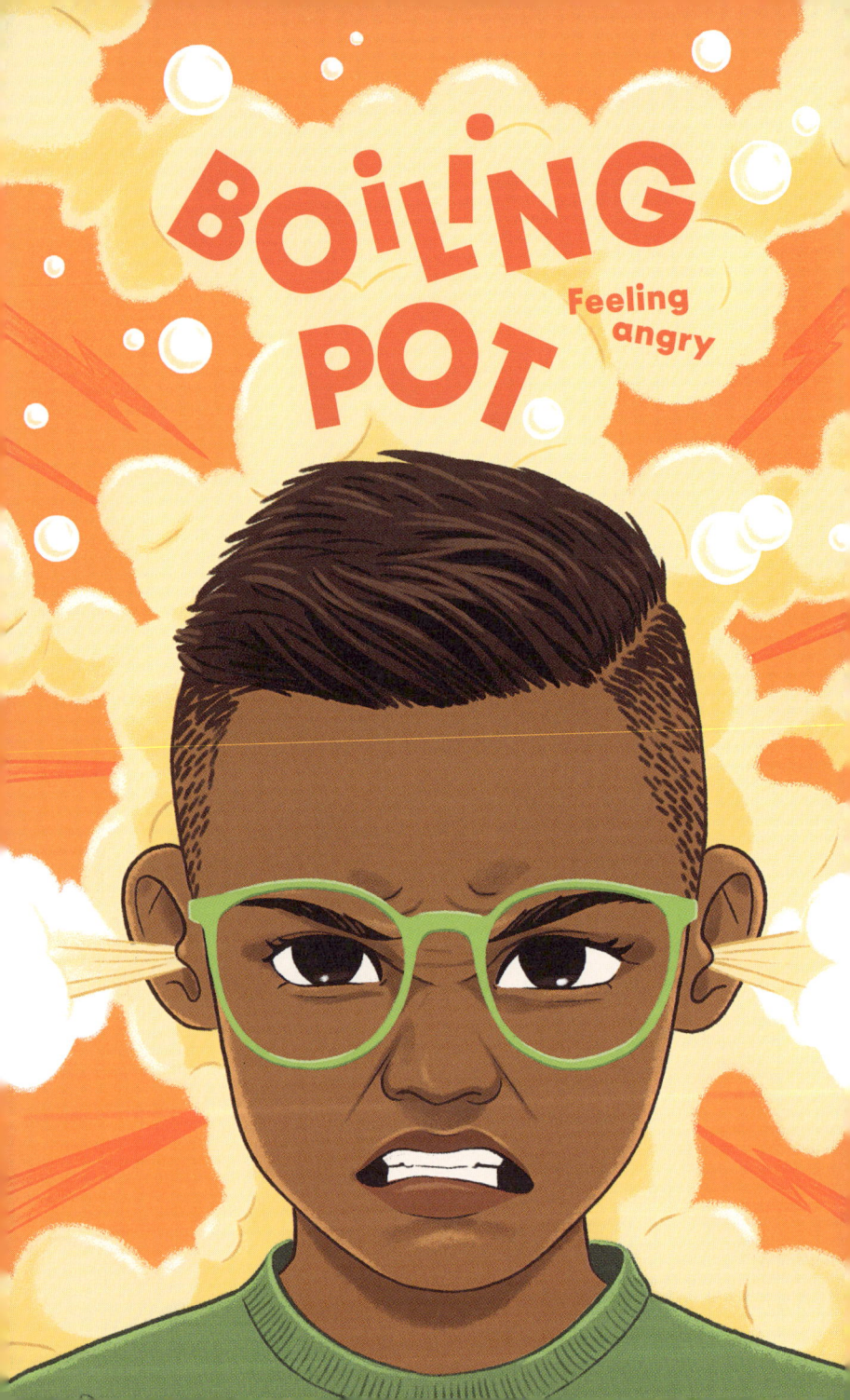

Anger's like a boiling pot,
You know what to expect.
Your troubled bubbles spit and pop
As energy ejects.

And if the heat beneath
Is turned too high or left unchecked,
You start to boil over
As the pressure takes effect.

But the thing about hot water,
Once you take it off the heat,
Is that soon those angry bubbles
Start to soften and retreat.

And though still hot, the bubbling stops,
Your temperature resets,
As you settle to a simmer,
And start feeling less upset.

And once your water's calmer,
You can finally reflect,
And make the right decision
On what action to take next.

THE PERSON YOU BECOME

Feeling proud

Win or lose, first or last,
Perfect score or barely passed.

Sometimes, no matter what you do,
The outcome isn't up to you.

But if you did your very best,
In any game or any test,

If deep inside you know you tried,
Then you can walk away with pride.

For pride is not about the win,
Pride's the effort you put in.

And if you tried, well then you've won,
No matter what or how you've done.

So don't count trophies on your shelf,
Just try your best and be yourself.

Work hard, be kind and have some fun
And be proud of the person you become.

PICKING UP THE PIECES

Feeling guilty

Sometimes something happens
That is not what you were hoping,
And you didn't mean to do it,
But something you love gets broken.

So you do your best to fix it,
Try to force it back in place,
But sometimes fixing problems
Might require some time and space.

And if you try to force it,
It can often make things worse,
So before you start to panic,
Pick up the pieces first.

Glue them very carefully,
Let each piece set in time.
And maybe that will right your wrong,
And the outcome will be fine.

But know that sometimes broken parts
Can never be put back,
And you can try a million things,
But you'll still see the crack.

And though it's hard to let things go,
Sometimes we must accept
That even things we truly love
Cannot always be kept.

HAPPY ANTS iN YOUR PANTS

Feeling joy

Joy makes people wiggle like a squirrel on a branch,
Or break out unexpectedly into a robot dance,
Yo-yoing around with happy ants inside their pants.

Joy can make them leap up like a kangaroo on springs,
Or flap their arms with open palms like albatross's wings.
Yes, they become a puppet, and their joy becomes the strings.

Joy makes people smile just as wide as smiles permit.
Open grins that draw you in and make you stare a bit.
Yes, isn't it a joy to see when someone's feeling it?

JUST RiGHT

Feeling loved

When there's love in your life,
Well, it feels... just right.
And whenever it's near you,
It fills you with light.

It's that cuddle, that kiss
When you're tucked up in bed.
It's a smile, it's a look,
It's kind words being said.

It feels gentle and fuzzy,
It feels like you've won.
And it warms your whole body
Like the afternoon sun.

And your heart starts to blossom,
Like bluebells in spring.
Yes, to love and be loved
Is a wonderful thing.

WHAT iF?

Feeling worried

What if I'm ~~not~~ good enough?
What if I ~~don't~~ win?
What if they ~~don't~~ like me?
What if I ~~don't~~ fit in?

What if I don't make captain
Of the school athletics team?
What if I ~~can't~~ understand
What the maths equations mean?

What if I ~~can't~~ do it?
And my friends think I'm ~~uncool~~?
What if things ~~don't~~ go my way
Today whilst I'm at school?

Inside every cannot there's always a can,
Inside every don't there's a do.
So when you say 'what if' when making a plan,
Choose the 'what if' that works out for you.

PLANET YOU

Feeling low

It's like you're in a spaceship,
All alone and lost in space,
And every planet that you find
Is a harsh and hostile place.

You're circling a black hole
And your engine's losing power,
No forcefield shield to fight the strikes
Of another meteor shower.

But look towards the darkness,
Do you see a speck of blue?
Right now it's many miles away,
But that is Planet You!

So turn your ship to face it,
Keep it firmly in your vision,
And make that tiny speck of blue
The focus of your mission.

Now start your engine slowly,
Build your speed up as you go,
And watch the way that day by day
That blue spec starts to grow.

And it may not be tomorrow,
Or the next day after that,
But keep your compass homebound
And one day you'll make it back.

And when you do reach Planet You,
When that speck of blue is near.
The fear of space will be replaced
By a welcome atmosphere.

THE GiFT OF GiVING

Feeling generous

If you have money
You don't really need,
Give it to others, do good.

For when you help others,
It makes you feel richer,
Than mountains of gold ever could.

THERE'S ALWAYS MORE TO LEARN

Feeling humble

Being humble's the ability to recognise your flaws,
It paves a path to help you laugh
When someone points out yours.

Being humble is accepting
You were beaten fair and square.
No bad excuse, no loud abuse, no damage to repair.

Being humble is acknowledging that even in success,
There's still some room for you to bloom
Before you reach your best.

Being humble is the knowledge
That good grades are great to earn,
But the brains that grow are those who know
There's always more to learn.

GREEN WITH ENVY

Feeling jealous

There's always someone somewhere,
With something you might like:
Creative flair, or perfect hair,
Or a brand new shiny bike.

Your eyes fill up with jealousy,
Your skin starts turning green,
Well... not actually!
But you know what I mean.

You start to solely focus
On that thing in front of you,
And you'll keep on feeling hopeless
Unless you can have it too.

But while you're looking longingly
At someone you admire,
What's true is you most probably
Have things they might desire.

Your happy smile, your summer plans,
Your new pet cockapoo!
And though it's hard to understand,
They could be jealous too.

'Cause nobody has everything,
There's at least one thing they'd swap.
So focus on the things you bring,
Not what you haven't got.

THE SECRET TO SUCCESS

Feeling determined

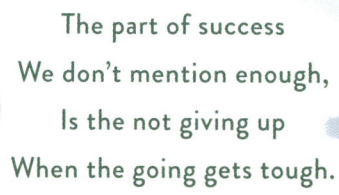

The part of success
We don't mention enough,
Is the not giving up
When the going gets tough.

Every someone you see
With a story to tell,
Has fumbled and stumbled
And tumbled and fell.

Not once, and not twice,
No, a great many times,
And they wobbled with worry,
Unsure of the signs.

But they trusted their gut
And they stuck to their guns,
And they never gave up
Till the doing was done.

So you see, there's the secret,
It's no magic trick.
Your dreams can come true
But they rarely come quick.

You must stick to your path
And work hard every day,
And refuse to give up
When life gets in your way.

And if you can do that
I would hazard a guess,
That sooner or later
You'll be a success.

LOOK OUT AT THE WORLD!

Feeling inspired

When you feel it, you'll know,
Inspiration is wild;
You can't keep it bottled
Or piled or filed.

There's no way to catch it
With netting or rope,
And it cannot be bought
With a hundred-pound note.

It is free like the sky
Or the wind in your hair,
And there's no way to know
When it's going to be there.

No, the best you can do
Is go out and be you,
And look out at the world
From your own point of view.

And when you see something
That makes your brain tick
With questions and queries,
Take note of it – quick!

If it fills you with passion
To try something new,
Or a deep sense of wonder
You want to pursue...

Well, that's inspiration
In front of your nose!
So follow it keenly
And see where it goes.

CLOCK-WATCHING

Feeling impatient

When I used to feel impatient,
And some waiting was in store,
I'd shuffle my bum and twiddle my thumbs
And pace around the floor.

I'd check the clock in case it stopped,
Then check my watch instead.
I'd race all sorts of silly thoughts
At speed around my head.

But here's the thing I noticed:
I could chew my fingernails,
Or wiggle and jiggle and squirm in my chair,
But it came to no avail.

9 10 11 12 13 14 15 16

Each second was a second still,
Each hour was an hour.
There is no way to speed up time
Without a superpower.

21 22 23 24 25 26

No, you can't make the clock tick quicker
By staring at each minute.
So fill each one with joy and fun
While you are living in it.

And you will find, time after time,
The secret that you're after:
The moments we are busy,
Are the ones that pass by faster.

29

31

32 33 34 35 36 37 38 39 40

THERE'S A HOLE iN MY SOUL

Feeling loss

There's a hole in my soul,
Since you left me.
Since you left,
There's a hole in my soul.
It's right where I kept you,
From the moment I met you,
But now there's a hole in my soul.

And it's filling with sorrow,
That hole in my soul,
With a sorrow as heavy as lead.
And I'm worried tomorrow,
More sorrow will follow,
Until I can't get out of bed.

So I won't let it set,
In that hole in my soul.
Whilst it's wet, I will let it wash through.
I will fill it instead,
With the life that you led,
I will fill it with moments of you.

I will fill it with smiles
That you placed on my face,
And the kisses I carefully caught.
I'll fill it with stories
You left in my ears,
And all of the lessons you taught.

I'll fill it with laughter
That bounced from the walls,
And the comfort of cuddles we shared.
With every warm look,
And the moments you took,
Just to make sure I knew that you cared.

Yes, I'll fill it with love,
That hole in my soul,
Until all of the sorrow has gone.
And you will live on,
In that hole in my soul.
In that hole in my soul,
You'll live on.

STARGAZING

Feeling awestruck

Stargazing is amazing – I can't believe my luck!
Whenever I look up to space, I'm constantly awestruck.
I'm standing on this great big ball of rock that we call Earth,
Floating with a billion stars, across the universe.

And as I look towards the sky and try to count them all,
I start to think that next to them I'm really very small.
But I'm also very lucky, I'm the one who's looking up,
And it isn't only counting stars that makes me feel awestruck…

It's jungles full of animals and trees that touch the clouds,
Musicians making melodies and playing them out loud,
It's storms that rattle windows as the thunder shakes the ground,
It's fireworks that sizzle, pop and sparkle all around.

It's robots and computer games, it's books and sports and food,
It's sharks and bears and dinosaurs, it's Netflix and YouTube.
It's sunsets over oceans as the waves lap on the shore,
Yes! Our planet has so many things that fill me full of awe.

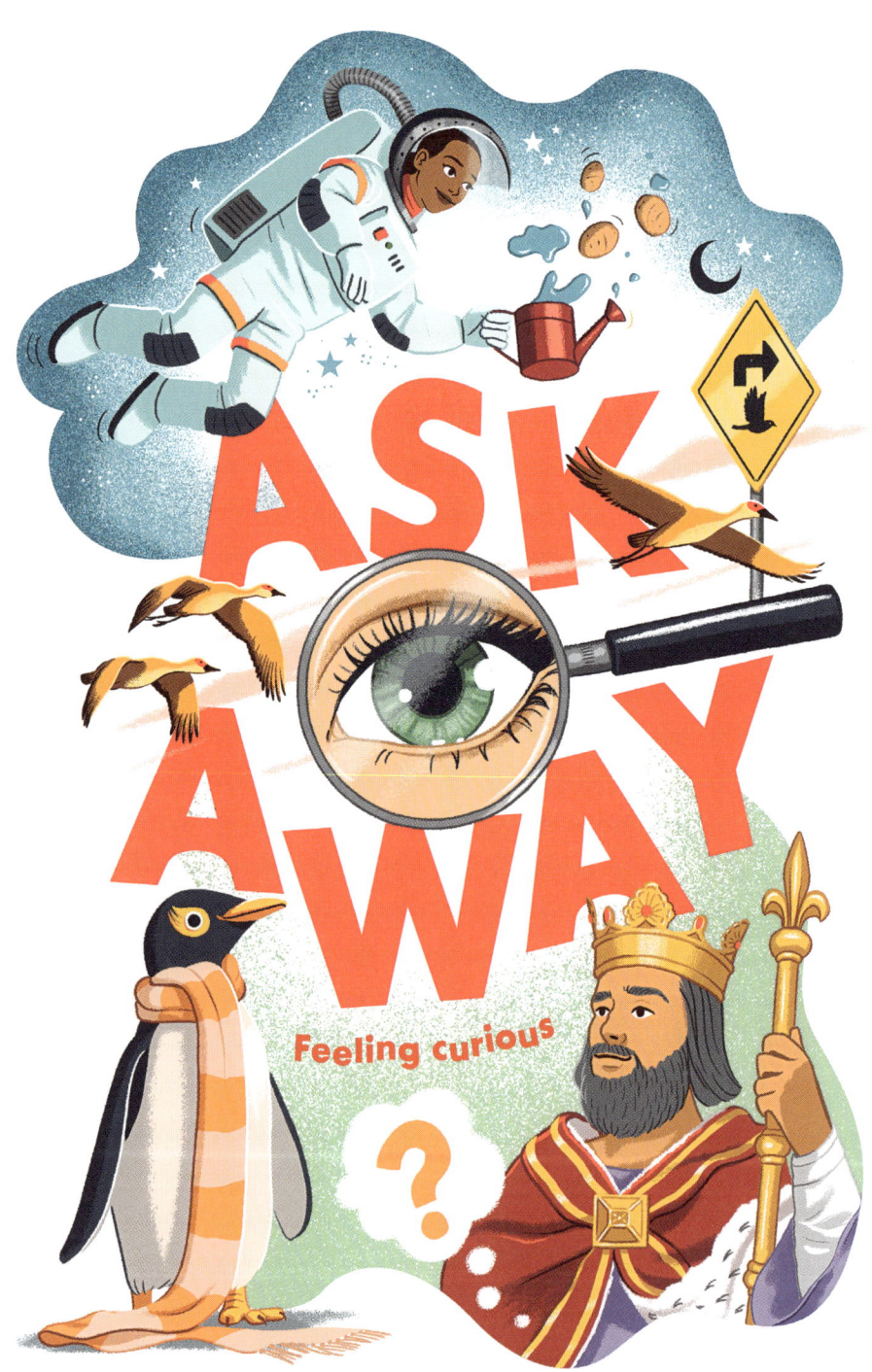

ASK AWAY

Feeling curious

What is **THE** world's tallest building?

What weighs **MORE**: a hippo or a rhino?

How long can **YOU** hold your breath for?

How do birds **KNOW** where to fly when they migrate?

Why is **THE** sky blue?

Are there **MORE** ants than people?

Is there a **YOU** in another dimension?

Can you **GROW** potatoes in space?

Why are there **SO** many different eye colours?

Can you **ASK** Google how to do a magic trick?

Why are there **LOTS** of different languages?

Are we made **OF** stardust?

What **QUESTIONS** would you ask a medieval king?

If you could live **WHEREVER** you wanted, where would it be?

Do **YOU** think penguins ever get cold?

Can people **GO** on holiday to the moon?

Feeling judgemental

SOMEWHERE

When two opinions think they're right,
They often cause a scene.
They scream and shout and jump about,
Expressing what they mean.

iN BETWEEN

And both believe they speak the truth,
But truthfully it seems,
The answer's rarely on one side,
But somewhere in between.

So just before you judge someone,
First hear their point of view.
You might have more in common
Than the lines dividing you.

BACK TO SCHOOL

Feeling unsettled

Dear Diary,
It's Monday.
First day back at school.
It felt so big,
And I so small.
It was nothing like my room.

Plastic chair,
Teachers stare,
Open window,
Autumn's air.
Wooden desks,
Books to share.
It was nothing like my room.

Time for shush,
Sit down, no fuss,
Work to do,
We're in a rush.
Walk in pairs,
Don't run, don't push.
It was nothing like my room.

But I was brave,
And I was strong,
And the home bell rang
Before too long.
Then I came back
Where I belong,
Back inside my room.

Dear Diary,
It's Friday.
Forgive me, I know
I've not written all week.
See my reasons below
Why I've not really been in my room.

We wrote a cool story
About an old queen.
I played my first game
For the basketball team.
We learned French! Bonjour!
Do you know what that means?
It means I've not really been in my room.

I made a new friend.
You would like him; he's ace.
We launched a pop rocket
And learned about space.
I sang in a choir,
I ran in a race,
So I've not really been in my room.

All week I was brave,
All week I was strong,
And I'm still a bit homesick,
Don't get me wrong.
But I'm starting to think
School's a place I belong,
So I've not really been in my room.

THE KEY TO FORGIVENESS

Feeling sorry

If you need to say sorry, I'm willing to bet,
You did something wrong that you came to regret.

And you may have a reason, you may have a why,
But next time it happens, here's something to try.

Simply say sorry, without adding **but**.
Then allow them to process the pain in their gut.

You may feel strongly you need to explain
Why you did what you did, and to clear your name.

But the **but** forms a circle, right back to the start,
And around you will go, with a weight in your heart.

No, simply say sorry for what you've done wrong,
And with luck they'll forgive you before very long.

Then after the heat of the moment has gone,
You can calmly express why you did what you've done.

Speak softly and kindly, and let them speak too,
And hopefully they'll do the same, but for you.

THE GiGGLES

Feeling amused

At first, I felt a tickle,
Then a twitch upon my cheek.
A chuckle started forming
Every time I tried to speak.

My lips could not contain my
Growing glimmer of a grin.
My shoulders started shaking
As I tried to keep it in.

My tongue began to titter,
My sides began to shake.
I let out a little giggle,
It was more than I could take.

So I chortled, then I snorted,
Then I cackled like a witch.
I hooted and I hollered
Till I gave myself a stitch.

But my laugh kept getting bigger,
And with one almighty roar,
I burst into a belly laugh,
And rolled around the floor!

TiME FOR YOU

Feeling relaxed

Find a hobby you enjoy,
Listen to **your** favourite track.
Take a moment on your **own**,
Or walk the extra-long **way** back.
What you choose is up **to** you,
Just find your own way to **relax**.

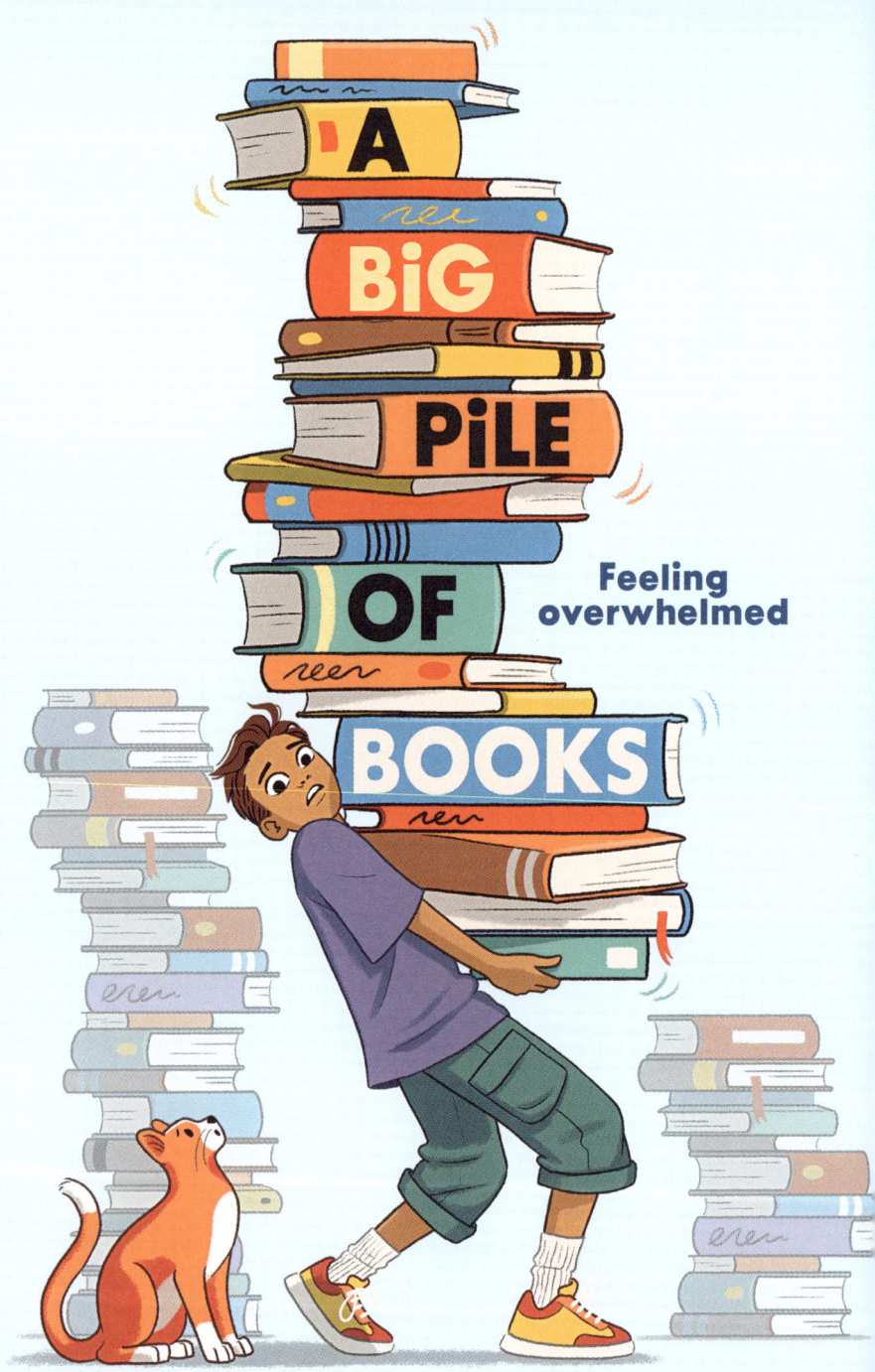

A BIG PILE OF BOOKS

Feeling overwhelmed

'Overwhelmed' feels like holding a pile
Of big heavy books for a mile.
And each step you take,
As they wobble and shake,
Makes it harder and harder to smile.

And your arms are now feeling the weight
As you strain just to keep the pile straight.
But here's what to do
If it happens to you:
Put some books down before it's too late.

And yes, your progress might be slowed,
But if you fail to lighten your load,
You'll come to a stop
Or you'll drop the whole lot,
As your book pile completely implodes.

No, instead pick the books you most need,
And walk on at a comfortable speed.
Put the rest in a stack,
You can always come back,
If there's something you still want to read.

BRiNG YOUR HAPPY BACK

Feeling grumpy

I was feeling very grumpy,
All the world was in my way.
I stamped and stomped and dragged my feet,
All around that grumpy day.

I was furiously grumpy,
Quite unreasonably mad,
With my bottom lip pushed outwards,
So the world knew I was sad.

I hissed and fumed, I snarled and sneered,
I gave my fiercest look.
I was very, very grumpy,
Not one thing could cheer me up.

That is until I saw a cat,
Who wore a coat and little hat.
I don't know why he looked like that,
But I started to smile at the way that he sat.
And the mood I'd been in, well, it started to crack,
Then I laughed and I laughed at that hat-wearing cat,
Till my grumpy was gone and my happy was back.

So now when I feel grumpy,
I don't let it ruin my day.
I just think of that cat and it makes me laugh,
And my grumpy starts fading away.

NO DOUBT

Feeling bold

The secret to confidence is rarely about
If you're good at the thing that you do,
But rather you do it unburdened by doubt
Of what anyone else thinks of you.

SHARE
YOUR
PLATE

Feeling
caring

If you're thinking about sharing,
Let me share a point of view.
Whenever there's enough for one,
There's just enough for two.

That is to say a plate that's full,
May fill your tummy's hole.
But share your plate with someone else,
And you will fill your soul.

So show you care, make sure you share,
With friends both old and new.
And maybe in your time of need,
Those friends will share with you.

WHEN THINGS DON'T GO YOUR WAY

Feeling disappointed

'Disappointment' is a sadness,
Found on the type of day,
When hopes and dreams tear at the seams,
And things don't go your way.

When you thought things might be better,
But they just don't go to plan,
And now instead, the day ahead
Becomes a battering ram.

And it hits you in the tummy,
Like a football at full pelt,
And drops you to your knees to plead,
For somebody to help.

But here's the thing to think of,
Whilst you're laid out on the floor,
You're probably no worse off today
Than how you were before.

You see, most disappointment
Only comes from expectation,
Of a thing you didn't have
Outside of your imagination.

So let the disappointment pass,
Get up and carry on.
Another chance will come along,
It's just this one that's gone.

And the next one could be better,
So may I suggest this:
Focus on the life you have,
Not the things you miss.

REASONS TO BE THANKFUL

Feeling appreciative

Your father, your mother,
Your sister, your brother,
Your family, your friends,
Being with one another.

A bird in the sky
As it glides overhead,
An ocean of blue
And a sunset of red.

Your favourite movie,
The books that you've read,
The songs that you sing
On repeat in your head.

Your trainers, your glasses,
The house where you live,
The hobbies you have
And the people you're with.

THE SUNSHiNE STATE OF MiND

Feeling positive

Make 'positive' a habit,
Whatever life may bring.
Good news, bad news, no news,
Find the good in everything.
And if you spot it, grab it.
Leave the rest of it behind.
Don't look for faults and issues;
Look for good, and good you'll find.

At first, it won't come naturally,
To smile when things go wrong –
And it doesn't mean you won't feel sad
Or must always be strong –
But you will find that actually
It gets easier every time,
As you train your brain in the subtle art
Of the sunshine state of mind.

BREATHE

DEEPLY

Feeling anxious

Anxiety's frightening,
It strikes you like lightning
And knocks all your senses for six.
Your pulse starts to quicken,
Your thoughts start to thicken,
Your heart becomes heavy as bricks.
But next time it happens,
Look out for the patterns.
Breathe deeply and ask yourself this...

Do you have control
Of what's taking its toll?
Could your actions undo what went wrong?
If so, make some plans,
It's in your own hands.
Breathe deeply, you've got this, be strong!

If you don't have control
Of what's niggling your soul
Then there's only the wisdom to know,
That no course of action
Can bring satisfaction.
Breathe deeply and let this one go.

NO-ONE iS IMMUNE

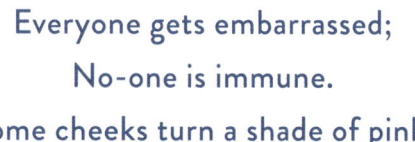

Feeling embarrassed

Everyone gets embarrassed;
No-one is immune.
Some cheeks turn a shade of pink,
And others, deep maroon.

From wearing jumpers backwards,
To singing out of tune,
Yes, everyone gets embarrassed;
No-one is immune.

From sharing art
Or a speaking part
Before a crowded room,
Or moments revealing
Your innermost feelings
Where fear of judgement looms.

Yes, everyone gets embarrassed;
No-one is immune.

Failed a test
Or made a mess,
Didn't go on the water flume.
Picked first, picked last,
Too slow, too fast,
Can't blow up a balloon.
Too nice, too mean,
Too in-between,
A voice so loud it booms.

Yes, everyone gets embarrassed;
No-one is immune.

So, if you feel embarrassed,
Don't worry, it will pass soon.
It's something that happens to all of us,
No-one is immune.

I like the days I do not know
Exactly how life's going to go.
When life's small collisions
Mean making decisions
From which new adventures can grow.

For sometimes it's in the not-knowing,
A new confidence begins growing.
And if you are bold,
You can let it take hold,
And all of the world begins glowing.

So when opportunity comes,
Don't be scared by the beat of its drums.
Say yes with a grin,
Let adventure begin,
And see what each new day becomes.

ON TOP OF YOUR GAME

Feeling elated

When joy is inflated,
 We call it 'elated'.
The height of your happy,
 Delight concentrated.

It's glowing with glee,
An excitement eruption.
A feeling of bliss
Without fault or disruption.

It's your birthday morning,
Unwrapping your gift,
And finding the one
You put top of your list.

Or an overhead kick
In the 93rd minute
That ripples the goal
For your team to win it.

It's pancakes for dinner,
It's Disneyland tickets,
A standing ovation,
That lasts several minutes.

It's pure jubilation,
No feeling's the same.
Those moments you know
You're on top of your game.

STAY TRUE

Feeling left out

Are you always sub at soccer?
On the bench for basketball?
Do your friends ride rollercoasters,
But you're still a bit too small?

Do you lack a certain confidence,
Or simply the desire
To audition for the summer show
Or sing in the school choir?

TO YOU

Don't feel bad, don't try to change,
Relax and be yourself.
Don't force a grin just to fit in,
You're meant for somewhere else.

So just stay true to being you,
Try new things with a grin,
And one day soon, you can assume,
You'll find where you fit in.

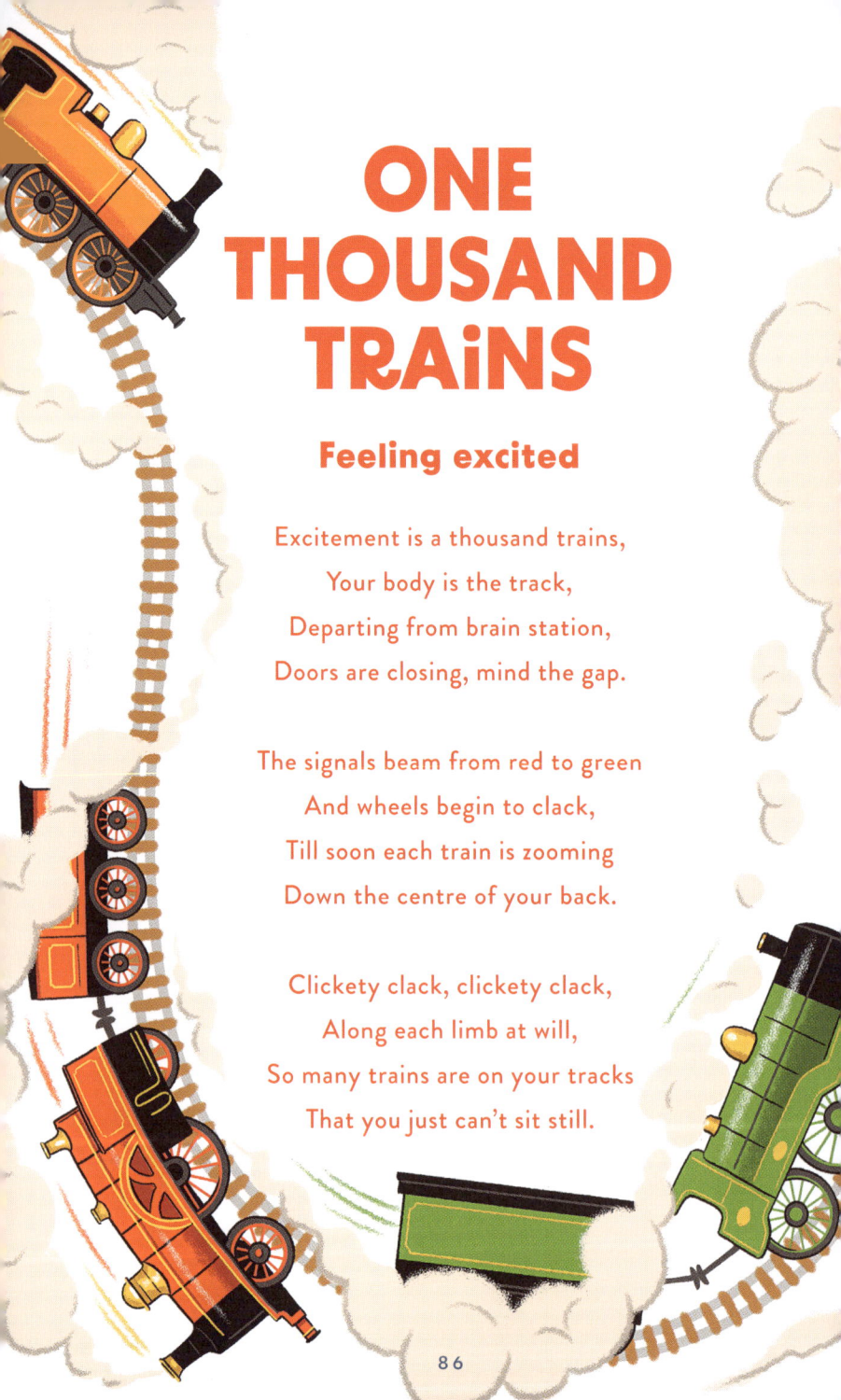

ONE THOUSAND TRAINS

Feeling excited

Excitement is a thousand trains,
Your body is the track,
Departing from brain station,
Doors are closing, mind the gap.

The signals beam from red to green
And wheels begin to clack,
Till soon each train is zooming
Down the centre of your back.

Clickety clack, clickety clack,
Along each limb at will,
So many trains are on your tracks
That you just can't sit still.

Clickety clack, clickety clack,
Your knees begin to jiggle,
Your fingers fidget frantically
And toes begin to wiggle.

Clickety clack, clickety clack,
Steam levels at their limit,
You start to think you might explode
At any given minute.

And so you shout or jump about
And let out your elation,
And soon that burst of energy
Sends trains home to their station.

They all head back along your tracks,
You feel the steam subside.
Excitement's not forever, so remember:
Enjoy the ride!

MAKE iT FUN

Feeling bored

If at first you don't have fun,
Then try and try again.
For fun is not the task itself,
But making it a game.

That is to say, if you get caught
In a mundane situation,
There'll be a way to make it fun,
Just use imagination.

So when there's rain, or days are plain,
That boredom felt inside your brain
Can be removed like socks and shoes,
If you make life a game.

Clean washing waiting by your door?
Free throw those pants into their drawer.
Two points per pair, and keep your score.

Your room's a mess? You need some space?
Pretend you're in a cleaning race.
You'll get things done at lightning pace.

Lost your bag? Don't feel dejected.
Imagine you're a great detective
And look again with a new perspective.

Just find a way to make it fun
And boring stuff will soon get done.
Then you should see, above all else,
There's always time to enjoy yourself.

THERE WILL ALWAYS BE TOMORROW

Feeling upset

If today was not your day,
If your heart felt full of sorrow,
If all the world stood in your way,
There will always be tomorrow.

If you felt fed up, or felt let down,
If it was just too much to swallow,
If no silver lining could be found,
There will always be tomorrow.

If you felt upset, or felt alone,
If you found no joy to follow,
If you wished all day you could go home,
There will always be tomorrow.

If it hurts too much to keep it in,
There's a phrase that you can borrow:
Don't give up and don't give in,
There will always be tomorrow.

I PASSED!

Feeling relieved

I took the test,
I tried my best,
I gave my all, but sadly,
Last night in bed,
Inside my head,
I worried I'd done badly.

I turned and tossed,
With fingers crossed,
I barely slept a wink.
And in the morning,
Tired and yawning,
I didn't know what to think.

I went to class,
My brain was mash,
My heart was beating far too fast.
I saw my test
Upon my desk...
I passed? I passed?!
I passed! I passed!

I felt the boulders
On my shoulders
Lift! And then I breathed,
So deep that I
Let out a sigh.
I've never felt so relieved!

BE YOUR OWN BEST FRIEND

Feeling confident

When you are filled with confidence,
You feel it in your chest.
A self-belief that sits beneath
And won't be second-guessed.

It's when you make decisions,
Based on what you feel is right.
You won't be blamed or feel ashamed
By the blaming, shaming types.

It's treating yourself properly;
It's being your own best friend.
It's not living the kind of life
Where you have to pretend.

It's being you entirely,
Every quirk and every charm.
It's a strong and clear confidence
Of peaceful inner calm.

It's knowing where your boundaries lie,
And where you shouldn't go.
Sometimes it means saying yes,
And sometimes, saying no.

It's waking up and treating you
The way you should be treated.
It's the confidence to take a stand
Without opinions needed.

Self-confidence is powerful,
And everyone can have it,
So wear it loud and wear it proud,
Like a badge upon your jacket.

LET YOUR FEELINGS OUT

Some days, the hours feel empty,
Some days, our brains feel full.
Some days are full of excitement,
And some are incredibly dull.

Some days, we wake and feel grumpy,
Some days, we wake with a smile.
Some days we're sad, then happy, then mad,
And each only lasts for a while.

Some days, we might feel lonely,
And others, we want our own space.
Some days we're grateful for things that we love,
But some days are harder to face.

You see, every day will be different,
No two can be lived the same way.
And because of that fact, the way you react
Will depend on your feelings that day.

Some days, your feelings come out with a shout,
Or a grin that is sparkling and wide.
But whether it's laughing or clapping or crying,
Make sure you don't hide them inside.

So cry if you need to, or stomp if it helps,
Try laughing or screaming or jumping about.
Or wiggle or giggle or yip or yelp!
But whatever you do, you must get it all out.

You see, like the forest needs sunshine and rain,
We too require fun times and moments of pain.
And some days it hurts, but the deepest of sorrow
Can help plant the seeds of a joyful tomorrow.

So share how you feel, growth requires every season,
And like our emotions, they change for a reason.
So don't keep them in; let your true feelings show,
And like seeds in the forest, you'll flourish and grow.

Published by Collins
An imprint of HarperCollins Publishers
1 Robroyston Gate,
Glasgow G33 1JN

www.collins.co.uk

HarperCollins Publishers
Macken House
39/40 Mayor Street Upper
Dublin 1
Ireland D01 C9W8

First Edition 2025

A catalogue record for this book is available from the British Library.

ISBN 978-0-00-872674-4

Printed in India

10 9 8 7 6 5 4 3 2 1

Publisher: Beth Rogers
Editor: Kerry Ferguson
Designer: Kevin Robbins
With special thanks to Amy Bradbury

This book contains FSC™ certified paper and other
controlled sources to ensure responsible forest management.
For more information visit: www.harpercollins.co.uk/green

MIX
Paper | Supporting
responsible forestry
FSC™ C007454
FSC
www.fsc.org